Rupert's Undersea Adventure

EGMONT

Early one morning, Rupert and Bill meet to play. "Look what I've got!" chuckles Rupert. "A stone with a hole in it. Mum says they're lucky."

Rupert and Bill want to show it to Ping Pong. As they reach her pagoda, they see her blowing a huge bubble.

"Bubbles here and bubbles there. Magic bubbles everywhere," chants Ping Pong.

The bubble doesn't float away, but spins slowly, floating in the air. "There," says Ping Pong, "bubbles that don't burst."

"Wow," leaps Bill, tossing the bubble to Ming. She teases the bubble with her tail, giving little smoky sneezes of delight.

Rupert and Bill head towards Rocky Bay. Ping Pong has a magic lesson, but promises to meet them later.

Meanwhile, under the sea, Miranda the Mermaid is collecting pretty shells for her necklace.

"I'm going to have the most beautiful necklace in the whole world," she says to herself.

On the seabed, Miranda sees something twinkling. "Oh, that's so lovely," she says, excitedly.

It's a beautiful, white pearl.

Miranda swims closer and closer to the pearl. "It doesn't seem to belong to anyone," she says, and reaches her hand out to take it.

Suddenly, it snaps shut! And poor Miranda is trapped inside. "GOTCHA!" says the clam.

"Ooooh, no!" says Miranda, frightened. It's very dark inside the shell.

Rupert and Bill reach Rocky Bay. "This will do. Watch," says Rupert, picking up a stone. He throws the stone, making it bounce across the waves.

A bubble floats to the surface, and from under the sea, Miranda cries, "He-ee-e-l-l-l-p!"

"Did you hear that?" asks Rupert. They both listen carefully. Bill throws his stone across the waves, and up pops another bubble.

Then they hear the voice again, "He-ee-e-l-l-l-p!"

"**D**idn't think my pearl belonged to anyone, eh?" says the clam, very upset. "Huh! I don't know. You young mermaids, picking up anything you fancy."

Miranda feels bad for what she's done, but calls again, "He-ee-e-l-l-l-p!" As she cries out, a bubble bobs out of the clam's jaw and floats up to the surface. The bubble has carried Miranda's voice.

Rupert and Bill hear Miranda call for help again. "It happens every time you skim a stone," says Bill.

"**Y**ap yap yap yap!" Ming comes leaping along.

"Hey everyone, I finished early," says Ping Pong.

Rupert throws another stone. As it bounces across the waves, they hear the voice again, "He-ee-e-lp!"

"That sounded like . . . Miranda!" say Bill, Rupert and Ping Pong altogether.

"It sounds like she's in trouble. We have to help her," says Rupert, rushing towards the waves.

16

"**H**old on, Rupert," cries Bill. "We can't swim under the sea. We won't be able to breathe."

Rupert looks disappointed, but then his eyes sparkle as he has an idea. "Ping Pong, what about your magic bubbles? Could you blow one that's big enough to fit me inside?" asks Rupert.

Ping Pong never wants to let her friends down, so she starts to blow a giant magic bubble. "That's one big bubble," says Bill, amazed.

Ping Pong sprinkles the bubble with her magic dust. "It's ready," she says.

Rupert is nervous at first, but he bravely pushes his hand into the bubble, then his arm, and then his whole body. "Wow wow wow wow," Rupert's voice echoes inside the bubble.

"Me next, me next," says Bill. Ping Pong blows magic bubbles for Bill, Ming and herself. Ming is delighted to have a bubble of her own!

19

"**R**ight then, follow me!" says Rupert, leading the way. All four friends half-roll, half-bounce, half-fly towards the sea, and then safely go under the water.

Rupert points to a stream of bubbles rising from the seabed. The bubbles lead them to the clam.

The clam was sleeping and the bubbles were drifting out with each snore. Every time his mouth opened, Miranda tried to wriggle out.

"**L**et me out! You're a mean old clam and I don't want your silly pearl anyway," wails Miranda.

Rupert hears Miranda's voice, "Miranda? Is that you?"

"Rupert! What are you doing here?" she replies.

"We've come to rescue you," says Ping Pong.

The clam is not happy. "The Mermaid stays right here until she's learnt her lesson," he huffs.

24

Then Rupert has an idea. He starts to kick his bubble, falling from one side to the other, tumbling and bouncing along the seabed.

"Woah . . . whoops . . . wahey," laughs Rupert.

"Oh, I get it," whispers Bill to the others. "If the clam laughs, he'll have to open his mouth and then Miranda can get out."

But the clam didn't find Rupert's tricks funny.

"It's a pity we can't tickle him," says Ping Pong.

"We can't, but Miranda can!" says Rupert, excitedly. "You two distract him, while I tell Miranda the plan."

So Bill, Ming and Ping Pong begin to do cartwheels inside their bubbles, while Rupert sneaks behind the clam and tells Miranda to start tickling.

Then suddenly, the clam begins to giggle, "Hee hee, tee hee hee! Ooooh, STO-O-OP!" he yells.

And out pops Miranda! Beside her falls the bright pearl. As she picks it up, the clam cries, "That's my pearl! She tried to steal it. And now she's got it," he huffs, "so I hope you're all happy." And the clam begins to sob.

"Miranda, is that true?" asks Rupert. She nods, feeling very ashamed.

Miranda swims over to the clam, "Please don't cry," she says, holding out the pearl to him. "I should never have taken it. I am really sorry."

"**A**h . . . hmm . . . oh, well," says the clam, blushing. "That was all I wanted to hear."

Rupert brings out his special stone, "Miranda, would you like to have this for your necklace?" She is delighted and strings it on to her necklace.

Rupert, Bill, Ping Pong and Ming say goodbye to the clam and Miranda, and roll back to the beach. They hurry home, just in time for tea.

The End

First published in Great Britain in 2007
by Egmont UK Limited
239 Kensington High Street, London W8 6SA
Rupert®, © Entertainment Rights Distribution Limited/
Express Newspapers 2007
All Rights Reserved.

ISBN 978 1 4052 3194 7
3 5 7 9 10 8 6 4 2
Printed in China